Adele and the Whispering Garden

Polly Richards

Contents

Acknowledgements

To God, for the many graces and blessings He has given; too many to count. And who gave me the love of gardening and inspired me to share it with others.

To John and Mary Kelly, who taught me that I can do anything if I put my mind to it.

To Bill, in the movie On Golden Pond, Katharine Hepburn's character, Ethel Thayer, tells her husband, "Listen to me, mister. You're my knight in shining armor. Don't you forget it. You're going to get back on that horse, and I'm going to be right behind you, holding on tight, and away we're going to go, go, go!" For me, this line symbolizes our enduring love and support for each other over these three decades of marriage. I could not have done this without your support. I love you!

To Adele, since the day you came into our world, our life has never been the same for the better and we thank God for you every day! Thank you for being the inspiration for this book. I love you to the moon and back, around again and again!

Chapter One:
The New Home

On the way to her new home with her parents, Adele's mind buzzed with thoughts. "Would their new house be as nice as the one they live in now?" "Would she be able to make new friends?" "Would it be peaceful or noisy?" "What about the neighbors?" "Would they be nice?" "And would there be adventures waiting for her?"

As the family car turned the corner, Adele pressed her face against the glass, her eyes wide with anticipation. The tires crunched over the gravel driveway, and Adele bounced with excitement as the car rolled to a stop in front of a house that seemed to whisper tales of the past.

"We're here!" she exclaimed; her eyes wide with wonder.

Adele's new home was a tapestry of ivy and brick, with chimneys reaching towards the sky like outstretched arms welcoming them. Her parents smiled at her eagerness.

"Yes, Adele, this is our new home," her mom replied, stepping out of the car.

Adele hopped out and breathed in the view of the charming old cottage surrounded by trees. "It's... perfect!" she declared, already itching to explore.

The three of them stepped through the garden gate off the sidewalk. It creaked on its hinges, revealing a pathway overgrown with wildflowers leading up to the front porch. They walked to the old oak door. With its intricate carvings, it stood like a silent guardian of a thousand stories within. The air was filled with the scent of possibility as Adele stepped

into her new home. Her heart danced at the sight of the stained-glass windows that filtered the sunlight into a kaleidoscope of colors on the walls. Her eyes sparkled with anticipation, and her heart raced with the thrill of exploration.

With every creak of the wooden floors and every echo in the empty rooms, she couldn't help but wonder what this new chapter would bring. Adele was a curious, nice, and kind-hearted girl, always ready for an adventure, and this move was the beginning of a great, new one.

As her parents unpacked boxes and arranged furniture, their daughter flitted about in butterfly fashion, her energy contagious.

"Adele, sweetheart, slow down," her mom chuckled, gently placing her hand on Adele's shoulder. "We have plenty of time to explore our new home."

Unable to contain her curiosity, Adele slipped outside to explore the backyard, her sneakers crunching on fallen leaves. Her parents decided to follow, eager to see the backyard too. Adele noticed a patch of tangled vines near the backyard fence, hiding something mysteriously.

"What's over there?" she wondered aloud, tugging at the vines to get a closer look.

Her dad glanced over. "Hmm, I'm not sure. Looks like there might be a garden back there," he said, appearing behind her.

Adele's heart raced with excitement. "A garden? Let's go see!" she exclaimed, darting through the gate with her parents in tow.

The neglected garden stretched out before her, a wild tangle of weeds and bushes. But amid the chaos, something caught her eye. There was an old gnome statue just in a corner. It was made of

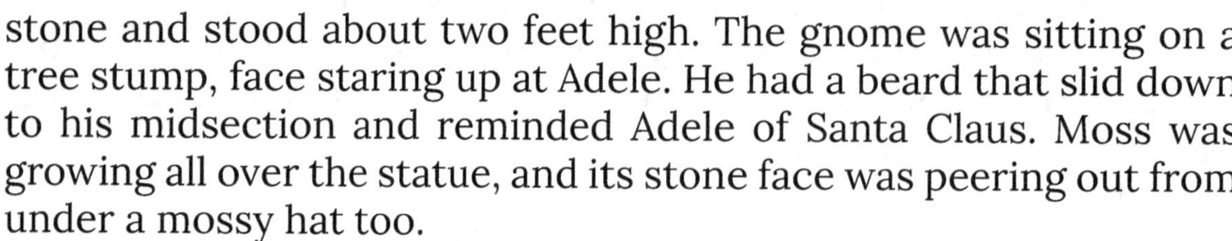

stone and stood about two feet high. The gnome was sitting on a tree stump, face staring up at Adele. He had a beard that slid down to his midsection and reminded Adele of Santa Claus. Moss was growing all over the statue, and its stone face was peering out from under a mossy hat too.

"Wow, look at that!" Adele gasped, rushing over to inspect the statue.

Her mom followed behind, smiling at her daughter's delight. "It's a gnome!" How amusing," she remarked, admiring the statue as if trying to guess how old it was.

Adele grinned from ear to ear. "The garden looks like it used to be magical and so beautiful. I love the gnome! Can we keep it, mom? Please?" she pleaded, already imagining all the adventures they could have together.

Her mom chuckled. "Of course, he can be our new garden guardian," she said, patting the gnome's head fondly.

Adele beamed with delight, her heart beating fast. She loved her new home!

The days in Adele's new home were filled with laughter and exploration. Every evening, after finishing her homework and dinner, she snuck out to the backyard to spend time with her new friend, the gnome she had named Albert.

"Good evening, Albert!" Adele whispered one night; her voice barely audible.

In the dim of the moon, she noticed that Albert's stone eyes shimmered, but she was not sure. She was not expecting a reply from the gnome, so she continued to talk.

"I wish this garden could be magical again," she confessed, closing her eyes tight, as if sending her wish into the night sky.

To her surprise, a gentle hum filled the air, and when Adele opened her eyes, Albert had come to life!

"Did you say... magic?" he boomed with a voice full of ancient wisdom, blinking his eyes in the soft glow.

Adele stumbled backward in shock. "You're alive!" she gasped, her eyes wide with amazement.

Albert chuckled, the lines on his stone face crinkling. "Indeed, young one. Your wish has awakened me. I was the gardener of this once-magical garden."

Adele's heart was racing. "You're real! This garden is truly magical!"

Albert nodded solemnly. "Oh, yes. Once upon a time, this garden was home to fairies, butterflies, and singing birds. It prospered with beauty, joy, magic, and wonder."

Adele became more and more curious and inched closer to the gnome. "Tell me more, Albert! What happened to the magic?"

Albert's expression grew sad. "Time passed and the magic faded. Pollution, neglect, and the fast pace of the world took their toll. The fairies vanished, and the once-colorful plants withered away."

Adele's heart sank at the thought of the garden's lost magic. "But we can bring it back, right?" she asked. "We can make the garden magical again!"

Albert's eyes brightened at the sound of that. "Yes, Adele," he replied. "With determination and love for the garden, we can definitely revive its magic."

Adele's face lit up with hope. "Can I help, Albert? I really want to see the garden's magic, and I would love to help bring it back to life!"

Albert's eyes twinkled with happiness. "That's why you were chosen, Adele. I've been waiting for someone with a heart as pure and determined as yours to reawaken the magic within this garden."

Adele beamed with pride. "I'll do it, Albert! I'll bring back the magic, and together, we'll make this garden the most magical place ever!"

Albert nodded approvingly. "I believe in you, Adele. Your journey has just begun, and I will be here to guide you every step of the way."

As she listened to Albert's stories and soaked in the magic of the garden, Adele knew that she had stumbled upon something truly special.

And so, under the moonlit sky, Adele and Albert forged a magical bond, ready to embark on a quest to restore the garden's lost magic.

Chapter Three:
The Garden's Glorious Past

As the stars twinkled overhead, Adele sat cross-legged beside Albert, eager to learn more about the garden's history.

"Tell me more about the fairies, Albert," Adele pleaded, her eyes shining with wonder.

Albert's deep voice rumbled as he thought of the happy past. "Ah, the fairies and the spirits were the heart and soul of this garden. They danced among the flowers, their laughter echoing through the trees."

Adele's imagination came alive as she pictured the tiny, shining creatures flying about the garden, leaving trails of stardust in their wake.

"And the spirits!" Adele exclaimed, unable to contain her delight. "What were they like?"

Albert chuckled fondly. "The spirits were mischievous little creatures, always playing tricks. But they had hearts of gold and a love for adventure."

Suddenly, Albert stretched out his arm to silence her. "Shhhh, do you hear that?" Albert said.

Adele stopped and tilted her head slightly. "It sounds like whispering."

"It is whispering!" Albert exclaimed. "The whispering of fairies and spirits. So, we call this place the Whispering Garden."

Adele gave Albert a smile of acknowledgment, listening to the sound of whispering floating in the air as they started to stroll in the garden, their footsteps echoing in the quiet of the night. They stumbled upon a sparkling stream, its waters shining under the stars.

"Wow, look at that!" Adele gasped, dipping her fingers into the cool water. "It's amazing!"

Albert nodded in agreement. "Indeed, the stream was once the lifeblood of the garden, nourishing the plants and providing a home for countless creatures."

As they ventured deeper, they encountered a riot of colors unfurling like a wave across the landscape—a kaleidoscope of flowers blossoming in every imaginable hue.

"Look at the flowers, Albert!" Adele exclaimed, twirling among the petals. "They're so beautiful!"

Albert smiled, his eyes twinkling with pride. "Each flower had a story to tell, a memory of a time when the garden was alive with magic and wonder." Albert continued to lead Adele through the garden, his footsteps softly marking the winding paths. "Each plant here has a special purpose, Adele," Albert explained. "They're not just ordinary flowers and herbs. They're guardians of nature, each with a unique, one-of-a-kind purpose."

Adele listened, hanging onto Albert's words. She felt a sense of awe wash over her as she realized the significance of the garden's plants.

"Take this lavender, for example," Albert continued, pointing to a cluster of purple blooms gently swaying in the breeze. "It's not just a pretty flower. Its scent can calm the mind and soothe the soul. It is a healer, bringing peace and calmness to all who breathe in its fragrance."

Adele reached out to touch the delicate petals, amazed at their softness. "Wow, I never knew flowers could do that" she exclaimed, her eyes shining in understanding.

Albert smiled warmly. "And over here, we have the humble dandelion," he said, pointing to a cluster of bright yellow flowers dancing in the sunlight. "Many people see it as a weed, but it's so much more than that. Its leaves are packed with nutrients, and its roots can be used to make tea that nourishes the body and boosts the immune system."

Adele examined the dandelion more closely. "I had no idea," she murmured.

Albert nodded, his eyes twinkling with joy. "Every plant in this garden has a story to tell, Adele," he said. "They're not just here to look pretty. They're here to heal, nourish, and bring joy to everyone."

As they wandered further into the garden, Adele could not help but feel a deep sense of gratitude for the plants that surrounded them. She realized they were more than just decorations; they were living beings with a purpose.

As they continued their journey, Adele felt her heart swell with joy. Albert captivated Adele with stories and the beauty that once existed within the garden's walls.

"Thank you for sharing these memories with me, Albert," Adele said, her voice filled with gratitude. "I can't wait to bring back the magic and make new memories of our own."

Albert nodded with warmth. "Together, we will make this garden glorious once more, Adele. The best is yet to be."

Chapter Four:
Fading Magic

The next morning, Adele was out of bed even before the sun had begun to rise. She couldn't shake off the images of the neglected garden from her mind. All night long, she had tossed and turned in bed. Her thoughts were filled with how she could make the garden lurking just beyond her bedroom window beautiful again.

Adele quickly, brushed her teeth, dressed, and made her bed. She then ran out of her room and down the stairs, her heart pounding with excitement and curiosity. She flung open the back door and ran across the dew-covered grass, her bare feet leaving tiny imprints on the damp earth.

Reaching the entrance to the garden, Adele paused for a moment, taking in the sight before her. Her face frowned as she looked at the garden. It lay still and silent in the early morning light, its vegetation wilted and weeds overgrown.

Looking around, Adele spotted Albert standing among the wilted plants. She went to him with concern in her eyes.

"Albert!" Adele gasped! "What happened to the garden?" her face full of concern. "What happened to the flowers, streams and fairies?"

Albert turned to face Adele, a warm smile spreading across his old face. "Good morning, Adele," he replied calmly. "Don't worry Adele. I used magic last night," his smile now looking impish as if he did something he shouldn't have. "But it doesn't last. Otherwise, how would we explain that a beautiful garden showed

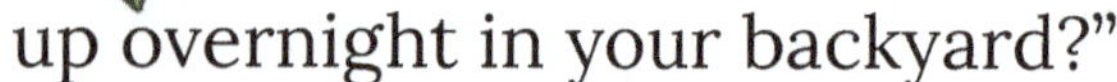

up overnight in your backyard?"

Without waiting, Adele followed Albert deeper into the garden, her footsteps disrupting the early morning stillness.

Adele was sad at the sight of the garden's state, but her determination only grew stronger. She would not let the magic slip away without a fight.

"What exactly happened to the garden, Albert?" Adele asked, her voice barely above a whisper.

Albert frowned and had a sorrowful expression. "Time has not been kind to this place, Adele. Pollution from the outside world has seeped in, choking the life of plants and driving away the creatures that once called it home."

Adele's heart sank as she took in the sight of the wilted flowers and barren trees. "It's so sad," she whispered, tears welling up in her eyes. "The garden was so beautiful last night."

Albert nodded in agreement. "Indeed, but all is not lost, Adele. With your help, we can bring back the magic and restore this garden to its former glory."

Adele wiped away her tears and squared her shoulders. "You're right, Albert. I won't let the garden fade away. I'll do whatever it takes to bring back the magic."

Chapter Five:
Adele's Quest

That evening, Adele was in the garden with Albert again. The garden had become her second home, and she couldn't get enough of it.

"Adele," Albert said, his voice grave yet filled with hope, "the fate of this garden rests in your hands."

Adele looked up at Albert. "I won't let you down, Albert. I promise to do everything I can."

Albert nodded, a hint of a smile gracing his weathered face. "I know you will, Adele. However, restoring the garden won't be easy. It will require patience, dedication, and a deep understanding of nature."

Adele's heart swelled with excitement. "I'm ready, Albert. Tell me what I need to do, and I will do it."

With a gentle nod, Albert outlined Adele's quest: research sustainable gardening practices, seek advice from knowledgeable gardeners, and gather supplies to start the journey.

"First, you'll need to learn about composting," Albert explained. "It's the key to nourishing the soil and promoting healthy plant growth."

Adele nodded eagerly, her mind already filled with possibilities. "I'll start researching right away! And I'll ask Mrs. Jenkins next door for advice. She has been gardening for years, so I am sure she can help."

Albert smiled, his eyes twinkling with hope. "That's the spirit, Adele. Remember, you are not alone on this journey. I'll be here to guide you every step of the way."

Adele wasted no time in her quest to revive the garden's lost magic. Determined to do an awesome job, she spent hours poring over gardening books and online resources, studying composting, pollination, and sustainable practices.

Every evening, Adele could be found curled up in her room, surrounded by stacks of books that her mother helped her find at the library. She had notebooks filled with ideas. She read every word, eager to absorb as much knowledge as possible.

But Adele knew that books could only teach her so much. To truly understand the art of gardening, she needed hands-on experience and advice from someone who had been doing this for years with expertise.

One sunny afternoon, Adele made her way to Mrs. Jenkins' house next door, her heart fluttering with questions and anticipation. Mrs. Jenkins was known in the neighborhood as a gardening guru, and Adele was eager to soak up her wisdom.

"Hello, Mrs. Jenkins!" Adele greeted her neighbor cheerfully as she knocked on the door.

Mrs. Jenkins opened the door with a warm smile. "Well, hello there, Adele! What brings you over today?"

Adele beamed, her excitement bubbling over. "I'm on a mission to revive the garden behind our house," she explained eagerly. "And I was hoping you could share some of your gardening secrets with me."

Mrs. Jenkins' eyes sparkled. "Of course, dear! I would be happy to help," she replied warmly. "Come on in, and we'll chat over a cup of tea."

As they settled into Mrs. Jenkins' kitchen, Adele listened as her neighbor shared tips and tricks honed over years of gardening experience.She absorbed every word, eager to put Mrs. Jenkins' advice into practice in the whispering garden.

Adele visited Mrs. Jenkins every afternoon for a week. She peppered her neighbor with questions, soaking up every bit of advice like a sponge. From the best time to plant seeds to the most effective pest control methods, Mrs. Jenkins shared her wealth of knowledge with Adele, making her feel inspired and empowered.

"Thank you so much, Mrs. Jenkins," Adele exclaimed gratefully. "I feel so much more confident now, knowing that I have your teachings to rely on."

Mrs. Jenkins patted Adele's shoulder affectionately. "Anytime, dear. Remember, gardening is as much about patience and perseverance as it is about knowledge. I have no doubt that you will do a wonderful job of bringing the garden back to life."

With the wonderful advice, Adele bid Mrs. Jenkins farewell and returned home, her mind buzzing with ideas and plans. She couldn't wait to put her acquired knowledge into action and begin the journey of reviving the garden.

Chapter Six:
Garden Guardians

One sunny morning, as Adele knelt in the soil, carefully planting seeds, a cheery voice chirped beside her. "Hello there, young gardener! "My name is Lulu, and I'm the friendliest ladybug you'll ever meet!"

Adele looked up to see a bright red ladybug with black spots fluttering beside her. "Hi, Lulu!" she exclaimed, her eyes sparkling with excitement. "What brings you to the garden today?"

Lulu landed gently on a nearby leaf, her wings shimmering in the sunlight. "I heard you were on a mission to bring back the garden's magic, and I wanted to lend a helping wing! Us ladybugs are pollination experts, you know."

Adele's face lit up with delight. "That's amazing, Lulu! I would love to learn from you."

Lulu became Adele's first garden guardian, teaching her the importance of pollination and role insects play in the garden ecosystem.

But Lulu was just the beginning. As Adele continued her work, she stumbled upon a timid earthworm named Squiggle, who shyly emerged from the soil to greet her.

"Um, hello there," Squiggle murmured, his voice barely louder than a whisper. "I... I'm Squiggle, the earthworm. I... I'm not excellent at talking, but I'm great at making the soil healthy!"

Adele smiled warmly at Squiggle. "It's nice to meet you, Squiggle! I could use some help with the soil. Do you think you could show me how to compost?"

Squiggle's face lit up with excitement. "Oh, yes! I... I'd love to help!"

Squiggle became Adele's second garden guardian, teaching her the secrets of composting and the importance of nourishing the soil.

But the most unexpected guardian of all was an ancient tree named Old Oak, who stood tall and wise at the edge of the garden.

"Ah, young one," Old Oak rumbled in his deep voice. "I have watched over this garden for centuries, and I have seen its many seasons."

Adele gazed up at Old Oak in awe. "You're amazing, Old Oak! Do you have any advice for me?"

Old Oak nodded. "Patience, young one. Nature moves at its own pace, and true magic takes time to unfold. Trust in the process, and the garden will flourish."

Later that day, as Adele worked diligently in the garden, her mind wandered to doubt and uncertainty. Despite her best efforts, she felt worried.

Lost in thought, Adele barely noticed when her parents approached to see how things were going.

"Adele, sweetheart, is everything okay?" her mom asked when she saw Adele frozen on the spot.

Adele sighed, her shoulders slumping under the weight of her doubts. "I'm not sure, mom," she confessed,

"I've been working so hard to bring the garden back to life, but sometimes I wonder if I'll ever succeed. What if I am not good enough? What if I can't make it magical again?"

Her dad placed a comforting hand on her shoulder and flashed her a smile filled with warmth and encouragement. "Oh, Adele, don't ever doubt yourself," he said, his voice gentle but firm. "You have a heart full of determination and a spirit that shines brighter than the sun. You can achieve anything if you set your mind to it."

Adele's mom nodded in agreement, her eyes brimming with pride. "That's right, sweetheart. Remember that even the smallest seed can grow into a big tree. You just have to believe in yourself and keep nurturing your dreams."

A spark of hope flickered within Adele's heart as she listened to her parents' words of wisdom. Their support filled her with renewed determination, making her doubts and fears disappear like the morning mist under the warmth of the sun.

With a grateful smile, Adele hugged her parents tightly, feeling their love and encouragement wash over her in a comforting embrace. She knew that no matter what challenges lay ahead, she would face them with courage, determination, and the strong belief that she could indeed bring the garden back to life.

As she returned to her work in the garden, a new sense of confidence bloomed within her, guiding her every step of the way. With Albert, the garden guardian, her parents by her side, and her dreams as her compass, Adele knew that anything was possible, and the whispering garden would once again flourish.

With knowledge and determination burning bright within her, Adele rolled up her sleeves and got to work, ready to bring magic back to the garden, one seed at a time.

"Let's do this, Albert!" Adele exclaimed; her voice filled with excitement.

Albert nodded in approval, his stone eyes twinkling with pride. "You're ready, Adele. Let's start by planting some native flowers, herbs, and vegetables."

Adele grabbed her gardening tools and set to work, carefully digging holes for each seedling and gently tucking them into the soil. "There you go, little plants," she whispered, patting the soil around them. "Grow big and strong!"

As she worked, Adele also set up a rain barrel to collect water for irrigation, ensuring that the garden would have plenty of moisture to survive.

"There, that should do it!" Adele exclaimed, admiring her handiwork.

But she didn't stop there. With Albert's guidance, she began composting organic waste which she would use to create a nutrient-rich environment for her plants to grow.

Albert said, "Compost is like making a cake. You have four ingredients, and you mix them together." Adele listened intently as he explained the process.

"The four ingredients for compost are brown stuff, green stuff, air, and water," he exclaimed, his right hand raised in the air, ticking off each ingredient with a raised finger.

Maybe this wasn't as easy as she thought. She looked at him with a blank stare. "What is brown and green stuff," her eyes narrowed in question.

Albert chuckled. "I'll explain. Over in the grass, you'll find dry leaves. That is an example of brown stuff." Adele went to the grass and scooped up handfuls of dry leaves, their papery texture tickling her palms, and placed them in the far corner of the yard.

Then, Albert said, "Remember when I told you to save the scraps from your kitchen? That is your green stuff." Adele ran and grabbed the bucket of scraps from the kitchen. They had carrot peel, apple core, banana peel, and ends of cucumbers. She brought the bucket to the compost bin.

"How do we get air, Albert?" Adele looked at him in bewilderment.

"Twigs mixed into compost provide air to pass through when it is all mixed together," Albert clarified.

Adele went over to Old Oak and asked if he had any twigs to add to the compost. "You've come to the right place," Old Oak replied. Suddenly, he started twisting back and forth in a dance, and twigs started falling all over the ground.

"Thank you, Old Oak! These will work out great for my compost ingredients!" Adele gathered up all the twigs and put them with the rest of the ingredients.

"Now for the water!" Adele said. She grabbed her watering can and went to the house to get water.

"Sweetheart, remember the rain barrel you put together. You can use the rainwater you have saved to add to the compost and water the plants,"

Albert said.

Adele's face looked like a lightbulb had just gone off. "That's right! I completely forgot!" she said, running to the rain barrel to gather water in her sprinkling can.

Albert guided Adele on how to make compost. He exclaimed, "You start by layering the dead leaves, the green stuff, the twigs, and sprinkle the water on top. Then, using a shovel, stir the ingredients together.

Adele stirred and stirred. "Now, do we put it in the garden bed?"

Albert's face lit up like he had forgotten an ingredient. "Oh, and don't forget Squiggle! He will bring his earthworm friends and they will live in the compost and help make it the best.

"Now we wait. Remember, gardening is about patience. Every week, we add more brown and green stuff, some twigs, and water. Then we stir it. Then we ask Squiggle and his friends if it is any good and they will let us know what we need."

Adele looked defeated, "How long do we have to do that for?"

"About four to six weeks. When the compost looks like dirt, you know it is ready for use in the garden. And remember, Squiggle and his friends are helping you," Albert explained.

For Adele, four to six weeks seemed like a lifetime. Albert smiled at her and said, "Don't worry, with all the other work you'll do in the garden, the time will pass quickly."

Six weeks later, Adele was on her way to add more ingredients to the compost bin. But as she started to layer the ingredients, Squiggle popped his head out of the pile. "We are all ready, Adele! Go ahead and add it to the soil!"

"All right Squiggle! Wow! Look at all this compost!" Adele marveled, stirring the dark, earthy mixture with pride. "I never knew recycling could be so much fun!"

As Adele tended to the garden with love and care, something incredible began to happen. The earth came alive with renewed energy and vitality, responding to Adele's efforts with bursts of growth and color. The garden gave off an earthy fragrance of moist soil as it mingled with the sweet perfume of blooming flowers. Adele had never smelled anything better than this.

"Look, Albert!" Adele exclaimed, pointing to a patch of flowers that had sprung up seemingly overnight. "The garden is returning to life!"

Albert smiled, his heart swelling with pride. "You've done it, Adele. Your love and dedication have brought back the magic."

Encouraged by the growth, Adele continued to nurture the garden, watching in awe as it flourished before her eyes.

Chapter Eight:
The Grand Reveal

As the seasons changed and the garden blossomed with renewed life, Adele felt a stirring within her heart. It was time to share the garden's beauty with her family and neighbors.

"Albert, it's time," Adele declared, her eyes sparkling with excitement.

Albert nodded; his stone eyes gleaming with anticipation. "Indeed, Adele. The garden is ready to reveal its magic to the world."

With joy coursing through her veins, Adele set to work, organizing a grand reveal unlike any other. She crafted invitations decorated with colorful flowers and butterflies, inviting everyone in the neighborhood to witness the garden's transformation.

"Everyone will be amazed," Adele whispered to herself, her heart racing.

On the night of the grand reveal, the garden shone with anticipation, its flowers blooming under the soft glow of the moon.

Adele stood at the entrance, her eyes shining with pride as she welcomed her family and neighbors with open arms.

"Welcome, everyone!" Adele exclaimed, her voice ringing out in the stillness of the night. "Thank you all for joining us tonight to witness the magic of the garden."

The crowd murmured in excitement as they gathered, eager to see what Adele had in store.

With a flourish, Adele waved her hand, signaling for the grand reveal to begin.

At that moment, the garden burst into bloom like never before. Flowers unfurled their petals in a riot of colors, their sweet fragrance filling the air. Bees buzzed lazily from blossom to blossom, and butterflies danced on the breeze.

The true magic came when the fairies emerged from their hiding places, their fine wings glimmering under the stars as they flitted among the flowers, spreading joy and wonder wherever they went.

Gasps of amazement filled the air as Adele's family and neighbors watched in awe, their hearts overflowing with happiness.

"It's beautiful!" someone whispered, their voice filled with wonder.

Adele beamed with pride as she watched the scene unfold before her eyes. The garden had come alive with magic, and she knew that its beauty would inspire and delight all who beheld it.

Chapter Nine :
Albert's Farewell

Later that evening, after everyone had left and the moonlight bathed the garden in its soft glow, Adele noticed a change in Albert. His movements became slower, and he looked different.

"Albert, are you okay?" Adele asked, feeling concerned.

Albert smiled gently. "Fear not, Adele. The time has come for me to return to my stone form. My purpose as a living gnome is fulfilled."

Adele's heart sank, a mixture of sadness and gratitude washing over her. "You brought so much magic back to the garden, Albert. We couldn't have done it without you."

Albert gathered Adele and her garden friends, the chatty ladybug Lulu, the shy earthworm Squiggle, and the wise Old Oak, around him.

"My dear friends," Albert began, his voice filled with warmth, "thank you for joining Adele on this incredible journey. Each of you played a crucial role in restoring the magic of the garden."

Lulu fluttered her wings, a tiny tear in her eye. "It was an honor, Albert. Your wisdom guided us all."

Squiggle nodded, his body wiggling with emotion. "We made the soil so healthy, just like you said."

Old Oak rumbled in agreement. "Nature's magic has a way of healing, and together, we've witnessed its power."

Adele wiped away a tear, her voice trembling. "Thank you,

Albert, for everything. I'll miss you."

Albert reached out and patted Adele's shoulder. "You are a true guardian of the garden, Adele. Nature's magic thrives when we care, and I have no doubt you'll continue to nurture this special place."

As the first light of dawn approached, Albert's form began to change. His once lively eyes turned back to stone, and his movements became statuesque.

"I'll miss you all," Albert whispered, his voice echoing in the stillness.

With a final, fond farewell, Albert returned to his stone form, his gnome features frozen in a serene smile. The garden, bathed in the twilight, was proof that magic had been restored.

Adele and friends stood in a moment of silent reflection, feeling the presence of Albert's spirit within the garden.

"We'll never forget you, Albert," Adele said, her voice carrying a promise to cherish the magic he had shared.

With that, Adele embraced her role as the garden's guardian, inspired by Albert's wisdom and grateful for the magic that had been reborn in the whispering garden.

Chapter Ten:

A New Beginning

As the sun rose with a new day, Adele stood at the heart of the whispering garden, filled with gratitude and pride. Albert may have returned to his stone form, but his spirit lived on in the magic that surrounded them.

"I promise to be the best guardian the garden could ever ask for," Adele whispered, her words carried on the morning breeze.

With each passing day, Adele tended to the garden with love and care, watching as it flourished under her gentle touch. However, she knew that the magic of the garden was meant to be shared, so she reached out to her friends and neighbors, inviting them to join her in caring for the special place.

"Come and see the wonders of the whispering garden," Adele called out. "There's so much to discover!"

Soon, children from all over the neighborhood gathered in the garden, their eyes wide with wonder as Adele shared its secrets and wonders with them.

"Did you know that butterflies drink nectar from flowers?" Adele exclaimed, pointing to a patch of blooms. "And that ladybugs are great helpers in the garden because they eat pests?"

The children gasped in amazement and became more curious as they listened to Adele's words.

"I want to help too!" one child exclaimed, reaching out to pluck a weed from the ground.

Adele smiled warmly, her heart swelling with pride. "Together, we can make the garden even more magical!"

With laughter and joy ringing through the air, Adele and her friends worked side by side, tending to the garden and nurturing its magic for future generations to enjoy.

"You see, each of you can be a guardian of this magical place," Adele encouraged, her eyes twinkling with inspiration. "Just like Albert guided me, you can help the garden thrive and share its magic with the world."

As the day drew to a close and the children bid farewell to the garden, Adele looked out over the whispering garden, feeling a sense of peace and fulfillment wash over.

As the stars twinkled overhead, the garden whispered back, filling Adele's heart with hope and joy, knowing that she had helped bring a little piece of magic into the world.

Seasons changed, and more children joined Adele in caring for the garden. Together, they planted seeds, tended to the soil, and watched as the fairies play, their delicate wings glowing in the sunlight.

On one special evening, Adele stood at the garden's entrance, looking out to the whispering garden. She knew that its secrets would be passed down through generations. The garden had become a source of hope, a reminder that with care and dedication, even the magic of gardens could be revived.

With that, she turned to her friends, both old and new, and together, they walked away from the garden, leaving it bathed in the shimmer of the setting sun. The magic lived on, carried in the hearts of those who had cared for it and in the laughter of the children who would continue the legacy.

"And so," Adele, feeling grateful, looked at the sky and said, "the whispering

garden whispers hope to all who listen."

THE END.

Pollution is when things that can hurt our environment, such as trash or smoke, mix into the air, water, or ground. It's like when someone makes a mess in our room and doesn't clean it up. This mess can also make it hard for plants, animals, and people to stay healthy and happy.

Sustainability is about using things that the Earth gives us in a way that makes sure there is enough for everyone, even people who will live on Earth many years from now. It's like making sure there's enough slices of cake at a party so that everyone gets a piece, not just the first few people in line.

Composting is a magical way of recycling our food scraps and yard waste, like banana peels and fallen leaves. We put them in a special bin, and over time, they turn into rich soil that can help new plants grow. It's nature's way of reusing things to help our gardens and the Earth.

Organic waste is like the leftovers from nature's big dinner party! Imagine all the bits of fruits, vegetables, and plants that you don't use when you're cooking. Well, those leftovers, along with things like eggshells and even some types of paper, are what we call organic waste. It's stuff that came from living things like plants and animals. But instead of tossing it in the trash, we can recycle it in a special way to make new things grow, such as compost for gardens.

So, organic waste might seem like garbage, but it's actually super important for helping our planet stay healthy and green!

How to Compost

Composting is like magic for your garden! Here's how you can do it:

Find a Spot

Pick a spot in your backyard for your compost pile or bin. Shady areas are best as they help keep the compost moist. Make sure your spot is easily accessible.

Get Your Ingredients

You'll need four main ingredients for your compost.
- Brown stuff: This can be dried leaves, straw, or shredded paper. Collect these from your yard or ask your family to save some for you.
- Green stuff: These are your kitchen scraps like fruit and vegetable peels, coffee grounds, and eggshells. Keep a small bucket or container in your kitchen to collect them.
- Air: To help your compost break down, you need air. This comes from mixing everything up regularly. Sticks help too!
- Water: Your compost needs to stay moist, like a wrung-out sponge. Use a watering can or hose to add water when it starts to dry out.

Layer it Up

Start by adding a layer of brown stuff to the bottom of your compost bin. Then add a layer of green stuff on top. Keep layering until your bin is about half full.

Mix it Up

Using a shovel or pitchfork, give your compost a good mix. This helps the air get in and speeds up the composting process.

Keep it Moist

Check your compost regularly to make sure it's not too dry or too wet. If it's dry, add some water. If it's too wet, add more brown stuff to balance it out.

Wait With Patience

Composting takes time, so be patient! Keep adding more brown and green stuff to your compost bin every week and give it a mix. In about four to six weeks, your compost will start to look like dark, crumbly soil.

Use Your Compost

Once your compost is ready, you can use it to enrich your garden soil. Spread it around your plants or mix it into the soil before planting new ones. Your plants will love the extra nutrients!

Remember, composting is a fun way to help the environment and make your garden thrive. Have fun experimenting with different ingredients and watching your compost turn into black gold for your plants!

olly Richards is a passionate gardener who resides in the northwest suburbs of Chicago with her husband Bill, their daughter Adele, and their two beloved dogs, Scotty and Olive.

In addition to tending her own garden, she manages a garden for her church, where an average of 2,000 pounds of fresh produce is lovingly grown and donated to the St. Vincent de Paul Food Pantry.

Her love for gardening led her to explore various approaches, from organic gardening to companion planting and the use of friendly bugs, such as ladybugs, to handle pests and promote pollination. She is on a mission to share these methods, whether for a blooming flower garden or a bountiful vegetable patch.

Polly firmly believes that we are the caretakers of this planet, a responsibility bestowed upon us by God. Saddened by the lack of concern for sustainable living, she decided to spark change at the grassroots level, starting with children. This inspired her to create the series 'Adele and the Whispering Garden'.

Thank You

Dear Reader,

Thank you so much for purchasing and reading this book. Your support means the world to me.

I sincerely hope that you enjoyed the journey we embarked on together through these pages. It was my pleasure to share this story with you, and I hope it has touched you in some way.

If you enjoyed the book, I kindly ask you to consider leaving a review on Amazon. Your feedback not only helps me improve, but also helps other readers discover this book. Remember, every single review makes a difference!

Once again, thank you for your time and support. I look forward to sharing more stories with you in the future.

Best Wishes,
Polly Richards